Pencil Magic

Written by **Gail Minthorn**

Illustrated by **Roxanne Ressler**

One Sunday morning
Nate found a red pencil
at the playground.
By Sunday afternoon
he knew the pencil was magic.

On Monday Nate took the pencil
to school.

His doodles turned into a work of art.

"Oh, Nate, this is super,"
said the art teacher.

And she hung Nate's picture up
right away.

At math time, Nate added numbers
faster than anyone else in his class.
All his answers were right.
"Good job, Nate," said his teacher.
She put a happy face on his paper.

After lunch, Nate wrote the best story
he had ever written.
"May I read this to the class, Nate?"
his teacher asked.
Nate nodded his head.
The class clapped when the story ended.

On Tuesday Nate carried the red pencil

to his softball game.

He rubbed it, put it in his shirt pocket,

and hit a home run.

"Wow!" said the coach

as Nate ran the bases and tagged home plate.

Nate used the pencil

to do his homework on Wednesday.

He finished the work so fast

that his mother said, "Done already?

May I see it, please?"

It was such good work

that she shook her head in wonder.

Thursday afternoon it rained.

Nate's pencil turned raindrops

into rays of sunshine.

Nate and his friends played outside

until supper time.

Friday morning
Nate dropped his red pencil
on the way to school.
He looked high and low,
but he could not find the pencil.
He got to school just as the bell rang.

Nate felt lost without his pencil.

But to his surprise,

he drew another fine picture.

He added numbers

and got the right answers.

He even wrote a funny story

about a boy who lost a pencil.

Nate was very happy.

Saturday came.

Nate's softball team was playing
its last game.

The coach said,

"Everyone, just do your best.

If we win, great.

If we don't, there's always next year.

Now get out there and play!"

Nate and his team tried hard
to play their best.

Nate didn't hit any home runs,
but he didn't make any mistakes.

The game ended and both teams cheered.

On Monday morning
Kate found a red pencil
on her way to school.
By Monday afternoon
she knew the pencil was magic.